Who Is Tapping At My Window?

for Lucia,
Laura, and Bruce

Who Is Tapping At My Window?

by A. G. DEMING • pictures by MONICA WELLINGTON

A PUFFIN UNICORN

Who is tapping at my window?

"It's not I," said the cat.

"It's not I," said the rat.

"It's not I," said the wren.

"It's not I," said the hen.

"It's not I," said the fox.

"It's not I," said the ox.

"It's not I," said the loon.

"It's not I," said the raccoon.

"It's not I," said the cony.

"It's not I," said the pony.

"It's not I," said the dog.

"It's not I," said the frog.

"It's not I," said the bear.

"It's not I," said the hare.

Who is tapping at my window?

"It is I," said the rain,

"tapping at your windowpane."

All possible care has been taken to trace ownership of and secure permission to print the original text of this adaptation.

PUFFIN UNICORN BOOKS
Published by the Penguin Group
Penguin Books USA Inc., 375 Hudson Street,
New York, New York 10014, U.S.A.
Penguin Books Ltd, 27 Wrights Lane,
London W8 5TZ, England
Penguin Books Australia Ltd, Ringwood, Victoria, Australia
Penguin Books Canada Ltd, 10 Alcorn Avenue, Toronto,
Ontario, Canada M4V 3B2

Penguin Books (N.Z.) Ltd, 182-190 Wairau Road,
Auckland 10, New Zealand
Penguin Books Ltd, Registered Offices:
Harmondsworth, Middlesex, England

Illustrations copyright © 1988 by
Monica Wellington
All rights reserved.
Unicorn is a registered trademark of
Dutton Children's Books,
a division of Penguin Books USA Inc.

Library of Congress number 87-30494
ISBN 0-14-054553-0

Published in the United States by
Dutton Children's Books,
a division of Penguin Books USA Inc.

Designer: Alice Lee Groton
Printed in Hong Kong by
South China Printing Co.

First Puffin Unicorn Edition 1994
10 9 8 7 6 5 4 3 2 1

WHO IS TAPPING AT MY WINDOW?
is also available in hardcover
from Dutton Children's Books.